For Alice and Manda — G.H.

For Leon, Matilda and Jude, my daring adventurers xxx — A.R.

First published 2020 by Nosy Crow Ltd

The Crow's Nest, 14 Baden Place

Crosby Row, London, SE1 1YW

www.nosycrow.com

ISBN 978 1 78800 883 9 (HB) • ISBN 978 1 78800 997 3 (PB)

Nosy Crow and associated logos are trademarks

and/or registered trademarks of Nosy Crow Ltd.

Text by Goldie Hawk

Text copyright © Nosy Crow 2020 • Illustrations copyright © Angie Rozelaar 2020

The right of Goldie Hawk to be identified as the author and of

Angie Rozelaar to be identified as the illustrator of this work has been asserted.

A CIP catalogue record for this book is available from the British Library.

Printed in China

Papers used by Nosy Crow are made from wood grown in sustainable forests.

1 3 5 7 9 8 6 4 2 (HB) • 1 3 5 7 9 8 6 4 2 (PB)

We're Going on a Pumpkin Hunt

Goldie Hawk

Angie Rozelaar

nosy crow

We're going on a pumpkin hunt.
We're going to find a big one.
What a beautiful night!
We're not scared.

Uh-oh . . .

Cats!

Watchful, green-eyed cats.
Can't go over them.
Can't go under them.
Can't go around them.

Got to go **through** them!

Meow, meow!

Meow, meow!

Meow, meow!

We're going on a pumpkin hunt.
We're going to find a big one.
What a beautiful night!
We're not scared.

Uh-oh . . .

Cobwebs!

Sticky spiders' cobwebs.
Can't go over them.
Can't go under them.
Can't go around them.

We're going on a pumpkin hunt.
We're going to find a big one.
What a beautiful night!
We're not scared.

Uh-oh . . .

Bats!

Flying, flapping bats.
Can't go over them.
Can't go under them.
Can't go around them.

Got to go **through** them!

Flap-flap!

Flap-flap!

Flap-flap!

We're going on a pumpkin hunt.
We're going to find a big one.
What a beautiful night!
We're not scared.

Uh-oh . . .

A house!

An old, dark, spooky house.
Can't go over it.
Can't go under it.
Can't go around it.

Got to go **through** it!

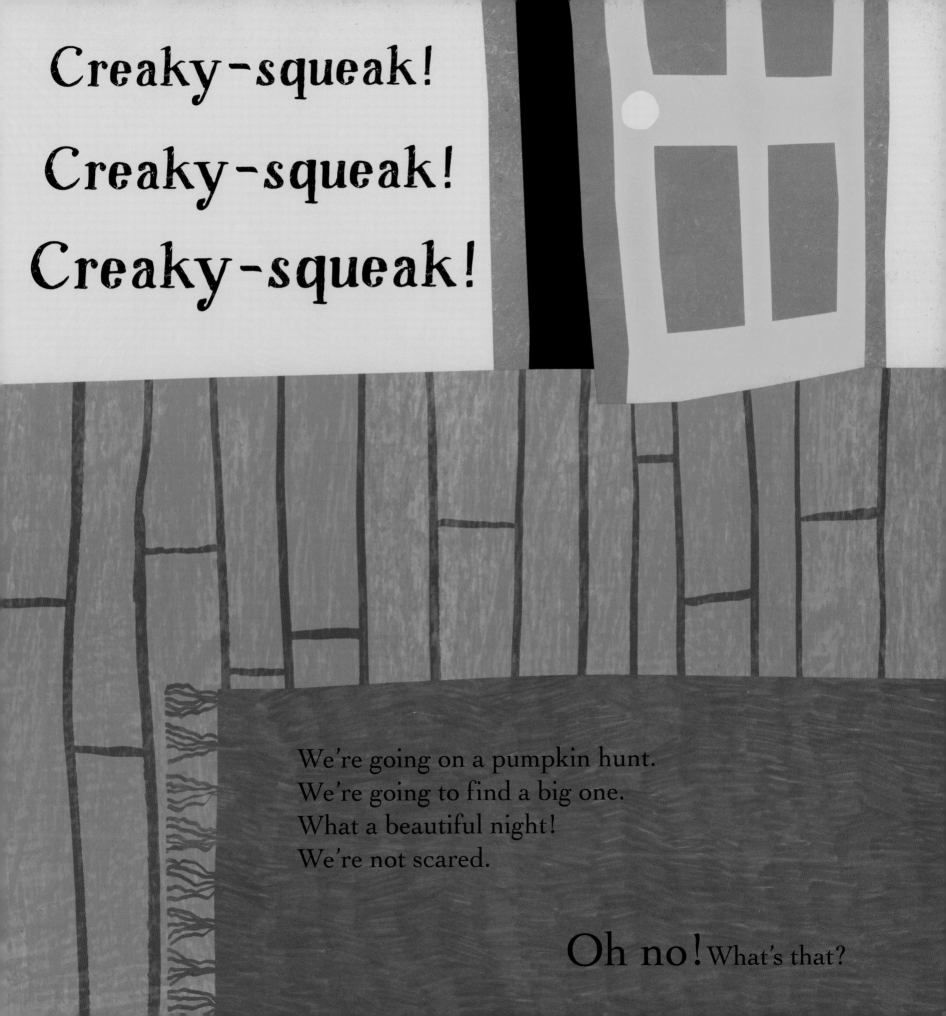

Creaky-squeak!
Creaky-squeak!
Creaky-squeak!

We're going on a pumpkin hunt.
We're going to find a big one.
What a beautiful night!
We're not scared.

Oh no! What's that?

Back through the house.

Creaky-squeak!

Creaky-squeak!

Creaky-squeak!

Back through the bats.

Flap-flap!

Flap-flap!

Flap-flap!

Back through the cobwebs.

Tickle-swish!

Tickle-swish!

Tickle-swish!

Back through the cats.

Meow, meow!

Meow, meow!

Meow, meow!

And all the way back . . . Wait! What's that?

It's a **PUMPKIN!**

Trick or treat!